D0674392

MADAME
PAMPLEMOUSSE
and the Enchanted
Sweet Shop

Also by Rupert Kingfisher

Madame Pamplemousse and Her Incredible Edibles
Madame Pamplemousse and the Time-Travelling Café

BY Rupert Kingfisher

ILLUSTRATED BY

Sue Hellard

LONDON BERLIN NEW YORK SYDNEY

For Rowan

Bloomsbury Publishing, London, Berlin, New York and Sydney

First published in Great Britain in September 2010 by Bloomsbury Publishing Plc
36 Soho Square, London, W1D 3QY

A CIP catalogue record of this book is available from the British Library

ISBN 978 1 4088 0505 3

Typeset by Dorchester Typesetting Group Ltd
Printed in Great Britain by Clays Ltd, St Ives plc, Bungay, Suffolk

3 5 7 9 10 8 6 4

www.bloomsbury.com

Chapter One

In the city of Paris, in the middle of the River Seine, there is an island called the Isle Saint Louis. To Parisians, however, it is also known as the 'Enchanted Isle', owing to its strange air of quiet in the busy heart of the city. On the Enchanted Isle there are no monuments or buildings of note, but instead shaded avenues, narrow cobbled streets, and a number of specialist food shops, florists and boutiques. And it was here that, one day, a sweet shop appeared.

The sweet shop was brightly coloured, with grape-purple walls, a peppermint-blue door and an awning of strawberries and cream. The shop's name was 'Sweet Dreams' and it was

owned by a woman called Madame Bonbon. A plump, buxom lady with rosy cheeks and a warm smile, she looked like a favourite aunt or ideal nanny; the kind of person you might turn to if you ever needed comfort. And comfort was just what the girl needed whom she found crying in Notre-Dame.

Notre-Dame Cathedral was a short walk from the sweet shop, as it was on the adjacent island, the Isle of the City. It was a cold afternoon in late January the day Madame Bonbon found the girl. The cathedral was mostly empty, with only a few lone tourists wandering through the candlelit gloom. There was a smell of incense in the air and also the faint sound of quiet sobbing.

Madame Bonbon found her in a dark corner of the cathedral's nave, sitting behind a pillar so that she was hidden from view; a girl slumped forward in an attitude of despair, her whole body shaking with tears.

'Oh, my little poppet, whatever can be the matter?'

At the sound of the strange voice, the girl started.

'Shh, it's all right,' whispered Madame Bonbon, sitting down beside her. She reached out to envelop the child in her arms. This provoked an unexpected flood of fresh tears, but Madame Bonbon rocked her gently until they passed.

When, eventually, the crying ceased, Madame Bonbon reached into her bag for a tissue.

'Thank you,' said the girl, taking it while

moving fractionally away. She had become embarrassed at crying on the woman's shoulder. 'I'm sorry to be such a nuisance. I should be going home.'

'Don't be silly,' said Madame Bonbon. 'You're not a nuisance at all. Now then, dear, are you going to tell me your name?'

The girl looked up at her with red, tear-filled eyes.

'My name's Madeleine,' she said.

Madeleine had stopped by the cathedral that day on her way back from school, seeking a quiet place where she would not be disturbed. She was in a state of great distress, but the source of her grief was something so shameful that she had not been able to share it with another soul.

'Thank you for your kindness,' said Madeleine, trying to break free from the embrace – the woman's perfume was very strong and she was beginning to find it suffocating, 'but I really ought to be going home now.'

The woman smiled, shaking her head. She did not move her arm from about Madeleine's shoulders.

'No, really,' said Madeleine, becoming somewhat alarmed. 'My parents will be wondering where I am.'

'Of course you shall go home, little poppet,' said Madame Bonbon, 'but not without taking a special box of my sweets!'

Before Madeleine could object, Madame Bonbon took her by the hand and led her out of the cathedral into the fading winter light. The wind had picked up and they walked briskly to avoid the freezing gusts, crossing over the water on to the narrow streets of Saint Louis.

Madame Bonbon's sweet shop was on the island's main street, tucked in between a restaurant on one side and a florist's on the other. It had a sign above the door with a picture of a crescent moon against a starry night sky. The moon had a face and was smiling. Sitting on his chin was a girl with fair hair, eating from a big box of sweets. Madame Bonbon removed a note that read *Back in five minutes* and opened the front door.

The shop's interior resembled a stage set from an old-fashioned theatre. It had high stone walls and wooden beams across the ceiling. The walls were hung with velvet drapes in shades of blue and purple, and were interspersed with mirrors, creating an illusion of depth. Lighting came from hanging lamps in the shapes of stars and crescent moons.

Next to the door there was a counter, with sweets stored behind it in tall crystal jars. Madeleine could see aniseed balls and acid drops, sherbet fruits and gobstoppers, caramels and sugared almonds, cherry lips and fruit jellies, jelly beans and fizz balls, multicoloured liquorice, a rainbow of lollipops, and bonbons in toffee, lemon and strawberry flavours.

The shop's specialities were arranged about the room in their own individual displays. These were in the form of miniature stage sets, with dolls acting out scenes behind a pair of blue curtains. There was a display for chocolate sardines, which consisted of a seabed with a mermaid sitting on a rock, combing her green hair. Another, for coconut-flavour toadstools, showed a winter forest, with little fairies and ugly pixies hidden in among the trees.

The most striking display was for

a kind of white chocolate truffle that came in

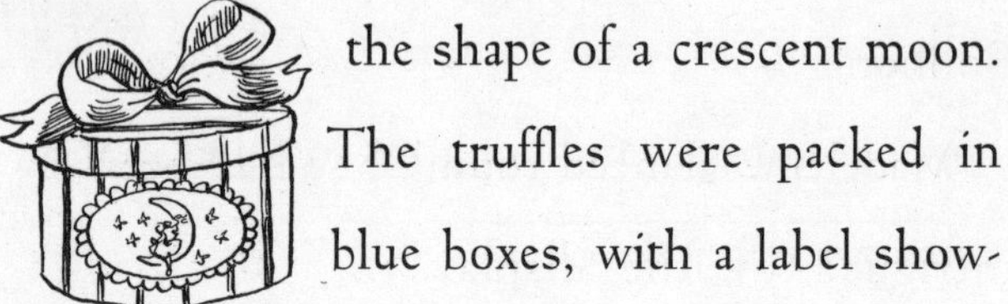

the shape of a crescent moon. The truffles were packed in blue boxes, with a label showing the same image as on the shop's sign. The little stage set consisted of a room that you peered into through the curtains. In the room there was a fireplace with flames made of orange paper, and a doll sitting next to it in a rocking chair. He wore eighteenth-century-style clothing, with a long, silver frock coat, stockings and knee breeches. His face was painted white and shaped like a crescent moon.

'Would you like to try one?' asked Madame Bonbon.

Madeleine glanced round. She had been so intrigued by the display that she hadn't noticed Madame Bonbon standing right beside her.

'Oh! No, thank you,' said Madeleine. 'I was just looking.'

'But I insist,' said Madame Bonbon. 'They're my speciality – you won't have tasted anything quite like them before.' She opened her hand to reveal one of the moon-shaped truffles. 'Here,' she said, handing it to Madeleine.

Madeleine thanked her and put the truffle in her mouth.

The outer shell was made of white chocolate and tasted richly of vanilla. The chocolate was quite solid and she had to bite firmly to reach the filling inside. This suddenly flooded into her mouth, some kind of velvety smooth liquid. It was sickly sweet and treacly, but with a bitter aftertaste. Altogether it was quite unpleasant and had Madeleine been alone she would have spat it out immediately – but just then she was surprised by a sudden onrush of joy.

Without understanding why, Madeleine felt radiantly happy. It was a bizarre feeling made all the more peculiar by knowing it could not be real. Only a moment earlier she had felt miserable and it was not that her troubles had disappeared, merely that she no longer cared. At least not for as long as she was eating the truffle. As she swallowed the last of it, so her old mood returned. Except now it was much worse. Earlier she had felt bad but there was a new edginess now, a sense of anxiety as if she were not quite herself. The feeling was dreadful and she knew the only way to dispel it would be to have another truffle straight away.

Madeleine looked up to find Madame Bonbon watching her. There was a strange intensity about her eyes.

'Did you like it?' she asked.

'Yes, thank you,' said Madeleine. 'It was delicious.'

Madame Bonbon smiled. 'Well,' she said,

handing her a midnight-blue box. 'Why don't you take some home. And then, when they're finished, you can come back for more. Would you like that?'

'Oh, yes,' said Madeleine, nodding. 'Yes, I'd like that very much!'

As she took the box, Madeleine noticed something peculiar about its label. The eyes of the grinning moon seemed much darker than before. With a slight shiver, she also noticed something about the girl sitting on his chin. It now struck her how uncannily like herself the girl looked, as if Madeleine had been the model for the picture.

Chapter Two

Before stopping in the cathedral that day, Madeleine had been on her way somewhere else. She had been going to visit two old friends of hers who lived in the Rue d'Escargot: a woman called Madame

Pamplemousse and a cat called Camembert. Together they ran a shop called 'Edibles', a delicatessen that sold all kinds of unusual foods. Some of them were very unusual indeed, as they were, in fact, the most extraordinary and delicious foods ever tasted.

'Edibles' was located on the Left Bank of the city, close to the riverside, down a narrow, winding alley. The shop's exterior was old and dusty, as if it had not been cleaned in many years. Inside it was lit entirely by candlelight. The smells as you came through the door were incredible: a heady mixture of old cheeses, sweet spices and drying herbs mingling with the sweaty, garlicky aroma of dried sausages and cured meats.

'Edibles' sold exactly 653 different varieties of cheese, including the first cheeses ever made and one from the Middle Ages that was so revoltingly smelly it had to be kept bound in chains and suppressed with a heavy weight.

Among the cured meats were sausages of Cockatrice and Pomegranate, Manticore and Stinging Nettle, Allosaurus and Black Pepper, alongside Whole Spiced Tyrannosaurus Claws and Honey-Glazed Harpy Wings.

Lining the walls were tall shelves packed with bottles and glass containers, with their contents written on the labels in fine, purple script: Devilled Chimera Kidneys with Habanero Chilli, Pickled Swedish Lake Monster in Horseradish Vinegar, Medieval

Black Truffles preserved in Unicorn Sweat, and Jellied Basilisk Eyes cured in Dandelion Wine.

Placed on the highest shelf and positioned in such a way that it would require a tall ladder to reach it, was a delicacy contained in a little jar. It had neither a name nor any ingredients on the label as both of these were a secret, since it was Madame Pamplemousse's special recipe, her greatest creation: the Most Incredible Edible Ever Tasted.

Madame Pamplemousse's shop was by no means famous in Paris. The reasons for this were mysterious, although the simplest explanation was that Madame Pamplemousse liked it that way. She had no desire for fame or to have hordes of tourists trooping through her shop, as this would have spoilt the delicate flavour of her wares. However, Madame Pamplemousse did have a number of regular customers, colleagues and suppliers, who together formed a loose company, a circle of friends. They were a group of philosophers and cooks, artists and musicians, who would often meet in secret beneath the streets of Montmartre. They met in a disused station, in what had once been part of the Paris métro, and this was why the group's members sometimes called themselves 'the Underground'.

Apart from Madame Pamplemousse and

Camembert, their members included the famous restaurant critic Monsieur Langoustine, the famous scientist Monsieur Moutarde, and a jazz pianist by the name of Monsieur Croque, who played music of aching beauty, but would only perform in the dark, since his face was so hideous. It was, in fact, so grotesque that some people claimed he was not even human but a stray gargoyle that had escaped from the roof of Notre-Dame.

The most recent – and youngest – member of the Underground was Madeleine. She had been recommended by Madame Pamplemousse, who believed that she needed

the group's protection, for she had detected in Madeleine the beginnings of a great talent: a rare genius for cookery that was on a par with her own.

Madeleine had been initiated into many of the group's secrets, including the secret of time travel. This was a discovery of Monsieur Moutarde, who had invented a device called the Taste-Automated Space-Time Déjà-Vu Generator. He kept this device hidden in a café, concealed as an espresso coffee machine, but on a certain setting it produced a liquid that could transport you through time and space. Last autumn Madeleine had gone time travelling with Madame Pamplemousse and Camembert. But since then a new term at school had begun, and Madeleine had not seen either of them since.

Madeleine had only started at the school the previous term. This was during a time of great change in her life. She had just moved to Paris after being adopted by a couple called the Cornichons and now lived with them above their restaurant, the Hungry Snail. But last summer, Madeleine had also become famous throughout the city thanks to her exceptional talent. The papers had called her 'Paris's new gastronomic star' and she had received many invitations to appear on television cookery shows. On the advice of the Underground, Madeleine would always decline these offers, in order to remain as anonymous as possible.

However, she found that her fame did have certain advantages, especially when it came to starting a new school.

Madeleine was not a naturally outgoing sort of person, but because she was a celebrity, people felt they knew her already. Everyone wanted to be her friend and all the different school gangs had invited her to join them. She soon made two close friends called Almondine and Cerise, who were themselves part of a larger group that used to play together in break-time. Much to her surprise, Madeleine found she was not only popular but one of the coolest people in the school.

But then the winter term started and a new girl arrived.

Her name was Mirabelle. To begin with, Madeleine made an effort to be welcoming. She sympathised with her predicament, having been the new girl herself the term before. She introduced Mirabelle to her friends and invited her to sit with them at their table in the canteen.

For someone new to the school, the canteen could be quite a frightening place. Madeleine had always hated it. Even though she had friends, she was always secretly afraid that one day they would desert her, leaving her to eat lunch by herself. But if Mirabelle was afraid, she certainly never showed it. She seemed perfectly at ease in the canteen and fitted into the group as if she had always been a member.

Mirabelle looked rather like a child model from the pages of a magazine. Madeleine could imagine her advertising Rollerblades, or perhaps a new brand of yogurt. She was dark and pretty, in a conventional sort of way, wore fashionable clothes and had perfectly cut hair. She was chatty and charismatic, supremely confident and the kind of person Madeleine had always wanted to be.

Madeleine had never been that confident herself. She was much too sensitive, always being acutely aware of how other people were feeling. But while this really ought to have helped her make friends, in practice it just made her more shy and self-conscious. Mirabelle, however, was not in the least bit shy. Nor did she seem to care whether anybody liked her or not, and, as a consequence, proved enormously popular.

In the time that followed, Madeleine would often look back to that first day of term. It seemed incredible that she had been the one who introduced Mirabelle to the group. It took a while, though, before it became clear that Mirabelle was trying to take her place. To begin with, Mirabelle was never openly rude to her or unpleasant in any way. It was just little things that Madeleine noticed; the way Mirabelle never quite seemed able to remember her name; or, when playing games, how she would always leave her out when allocating the teams.

Then Mirabelle began meeting Madeleine's friends after school, but would somehow always forget to include Madeleine. Again, Madeleine was never actively excluded. If she had been more confident, she could easily have invited herself. But then confidence was not Madeleine's strongest characteristic.

At first she kept wondering if it was just her imagination; perhaps she was being too sensitive. Except she could not help but feel that Mirabelle was preying upon a weakness. Madeleine had always felt slightly insecure in the group due to having no actual best friend. Cerise and Almondine were her two closest friends, but they had known each other long before Madeleine arrived.

By the third week of term she realised it was not her imagination, but by then it was too late, because that was when the real bullying began.

It started quite suddenly one freezing cold Monday. She had arrived late, in a fluster, having run from the métro. She went to her usual seat beside Almondine and Cerise and started telling them about her morning, but neither of them replied. She thought they had not heard and so spoke louder, but still they did not answer. Instead they looked at each other, raising their eyebrows as if to say, '*Who is this annoying girl?*'

As the morning wore on, so did Madeleine's state of anxiety. She was entirely unable to concentrate and when the teacher, Madame Poulet, asked her a question, she had to repeat it three times.

'The answer's not outside the window, Madeleine!' she said, much to the amusement of the class.

By lunchtime, the situation had worsened considerably. All Madeleine's secret fears about the canteen had come true. Throughout the entire lunch break, not a single person spoke to her. However, she felt certain they were all talking about her, as she could see people glancing at her, whispering and giggling.

That was the day when Madame Bonbon found Madeleine crying in the cathedral. But it was not the actual bullying that made her cry: it was the feeling of shame. She had wanted so badly to ask for Madame Pamplemousse's help, but realised she could not, for it was her disappointment that Madeleine feared most of all.

Chapter Three

The next day at school, Madame Poulet was leading a group discussion. She held these every so often throughout the term, on various topics such as 'friendship', 'kindness' and 'dealing with bullying'. This morning the subject was 'feeling left out'. Madame Poulet was talking about how sometimes you saw people in the playground who looked lonely or did not take part in games. She asked the class why this might be.

'Please, Madame,' said Mirabelle, putting up her hand.

'Yes, Mirabelle?' said Madame Poulet. Mirabelle was her favourite pupil and she always picked her out first.

'It's because they're shy, isn't it?'

Madame Poulet nodded approvingly. 'Well done, Mirabelle, that's right.' She wrote *SHY* in big letters on the whiteboard. 'Sometimes people want to join in but they can't because they feel shy, and these are the sort of people who need our help and support.' She paused. 'Now, there's nothing wrong with being shy, I'm not trying to suggest that. But shy people are often lonely. They want to fit in like other people, but they don't really know how. Now, can anyone tell me what other kind of children might have that problem?'

Several people put up their hand but Madame Poulet squinted until she found Mirabelle's again.

'Yes, Mirabelle?' she said.

'Children who aren't normal, Madame.'

Madame Poulet frowned. This was not quite the answer she had been hoping for. 'What do you mean by that, exactly?'

'Well,' said Mirabelle, 'it's like my dad says:

child prodigies are some of the loneliest children in the world because they're not allowed to be just normal kids.'

Madame Poulet smiled. 'Ah, yes!' she said. 'I quite agree with your father.' She addressed the rest of the class. 'For those of you who don't know, a child prodigy is a child who's particularly gifted at something, who shows an unusual talent or ability . . .' She paused to frown at Madeleine over her spectacles. 'Now, having talent's a wonderful thing – let's be quite clear about that – but not if it sets you apart from other people.'

This remark was probably the least helpful thing anyone could have said to Madeleine just then. She was already afraid that everybody knew what was happening to her in the group. She tried her best not to let it show, although during lunchtime this was practically impossible.

There was still a space waiting at her usual table in the canteen. Madeleine sat down quietly, not meeting anyone's eye and only half whispering 'hello'. Nobody seemed to notice – they were all talking among themselves. But as Madeleine listened closer, it soon became clear that she was the main topic of conversation.

It was rather as though Madeleine were an animal at the zoo. No one spoke to her, but instead they all pointed and stared. In minute detail they criticised every aspect of her appearance: her choice of clothing, her hair, even the way she was eating. Madeleine's plate became a minefield. She avoided certain foods in favour of others, so as not to incur mockery. For some unknown reason, bread seemed to be acceptable, while cheese provoked giggling and fruit reduced everyone to hysterics.

Halfway through lunch, Mirabelle reminded everyone about that morning's discussion. It was their duty to help Madeleine, she told them. They had to be supportive as a group because she was so painfully shy. Mirabelle said this in a patronising, head-girlish sort of way and then turned to Madeleine, smiling.

'Well, say something, then!' she suddenly

shouted in her face.

This would normally have made anyone jump, but Madeleine had now become so withdrawn that she just sat there impassively.

'Er . . . hello, Madeleine?' said Mirabelle. 'It's lunchtime! This is when people usually talk!'

Madeleine remained silent.

'I know!' Mirabelle cried. 'It's because she doesn't know what to say! She can't talk about normal things because she isn't normal – she's *special*!'

A titter went around the table.

'So come on, Madeleine!' she said. 'We're all giving you a chance. If you can think of something interesting or funny to say, then we might carry on being your friends. Or don't you want us to be your friends? Would you rather sit here *all by yourself*?'

This last produced a general gasp, a mixture of fear and delight. Mirabelle had just spoken aloud everyone's worst fear. Madeleine was trembling. If she tried to speak, her voice would start shaking and there was a serious danger she might cry, but what she wanted to do was shout. She wanted to scream: '*You know nothing about me! I'm a member of the Underground and I've travelled through time! I was nearly eaten by dinosaurs – do you really think I'm frightened of you?!*'

Unfortunately, though, she could not say this because it would have been a lie, since compared to these girls, dinosaurs hardly seemed frightening at all. Madeleine stood up, saying she had to go to the bathroom. She immediately regretted it. No one usually announced such a thing; they would just get up and leave the table.

Mirabelle noticed her embarrassment and made sure everyone else did too.

'Was that it?' she said, rolling her eyes humorously. 'Well, that was worth waiting for!'

There was a burst of raucous laughter. A hot flush went up Madeleine's neck and she walked away with her face burning, feeling everyone's eyes on her back.

Once she left the canteen she made her way straight to the library, knowing it would be empty at this time. She went to a quiet corner

and reached into her pocket, bringing out the midnight-blue box.

Opening it, she found there were only three truffles left. She did not realise how many she must have eaten. Now they would have to be rationed; she would eat just one more and save the other two for tomorrow.

The next moment, Madeleine had stuffed all three truffles into her mouth.

The effect was immediate and powerful. As her teeth bit through the outer shells, the liquid centres spilled out. The sickly sweetness was overpowering and the bitter aftertaste much stronger than before. The intensity of it made her head spin and her legs

LIBRARY

turn to jelly. Madeleine keeled over, collapsing on to the floor; except that now there was no floor, only a space of pure darkness into which she began to fall.

For how long she was unconscious Madeleine had no idea, but when at last she awoke she found herself lying in a bed. A large wrought silver bed with an ornately patterned frame. The sheets were icy cold as if they had been frozen, sending a deep chill to her bones.

She did not recognise the room that she was in. It was empty apart from the bed and both the walls and floor appeared to be made of white marble. Opposite her there was a tall window looking out on to the night sky. Beside it there was a door ajar, showing a faint glimmer of light.

Madeleine got out of bed and went over to the doorway to peer through the gap. She looked through it into a long room, like the great hall of a castle. At the far end there was a fireplace with a fire burning in the hearth. Sitting next to it was somebody in a rocking chair. She could only see his legs and shoes, both of which were coloured bright silver. The figure was sitting cross-legged, rocking gently back and forth. But then, quite suddenly, almost as if sensing he was being watched, the figure stood up.

To her relief, however, he did not turn round but went over towards the fire. He bent down, picking up a poker to stoke the glowing coals. His coat was also silver-coloured and sparkled in the firelight. All the while as she watched him, Madeleine had been holding her breath, but she could not do so any longer and let out a gasp. The figure did not move. He remained with his back to her, staring into the flames. There was no telling if he had heard her. Madeleine was just about to creep away when the figure turned round.

He had a face that Madeleine recognised from Madame Bonbon's shop: the little doll from the display, with the face of a crescent moon.

Now, standing upright, he was the height of a tall man. His skin was ghostly white and covered in thick make-up, with a beauty spot on his cheek and chocolate-coloured lipstick. As she stared at him, his lips curled into a cruel-looking smile.

Madeleine bolted back from the door and jumped into the bed. She burrowed in deep beneath the covers, pretending desperately to be asleep. But through the sheets she could hear the sound of footsteps echoing on the hard marble floor.

Chapter Four

Many years ago, before any of this happened, when Madame Bonbon was a girl of about Madeleine's age, she lived in a small village in Provence. It was built high into the hillside atop a crag of jagged stone. Its ramparts looked down over a wide vista below, a view across plains and lavender fields reaching out towards the sea.

Madame Bonbon's first name was Coco. She was a pretty child, with corkscrew blonde curls and cornflower-blue eyes. She looked rather like a doll and this was also how her parents treated her, dressing her up in charming frocks and putting ribbons in her hair. And, just like a doll, she was not expected to cry. Coco's parents did not like it when children cried, and if ever she did, they threatened to lock her in the cellar.

The cellar was dank and cold and smelt strongly of mildew. Coco had always been afraid of it. In particular she was scared of

something that she had once found down there. It was an old, rusty tin that her father used for keeping nails. Previously it had contained drinking chocolate and showed a picture of a crescent moon against a star-spangled sky. The moon was smiling and had dark eyes that seemed to follow you about the room.

One time when Coco got upset and would not stop crying, her father lifted her up over his shoulder and carried her down the stairs. Then he locked the cellar door and switched off the light.

Coco was kept down there in total darkness for two whole days and nights. After that she never cried again or got angry or upset, but learnt always to appear pretty and charming to her parents. But from behind her smiling mask she began watching them. Coco was very good at watching people and often just from watching them she could tell what they were thinking. She had a knack for finding out people's secrets, their hidden fears and desires. She knew her father's desire was to be rich and this is why he squirrelled money away beneath the floorboards of his study. And she knew her mother's secret wish was to be somewhere far away from both her husband and daughter.

Coco's house was always dirty, everywhere covered in dust and a thin layer of grime. This was because her mother was too lazy to do any housework, and her father was too mean to afford a proper cleaner. But one day Coco's father had an ingenious idea: he would adopt a child. A strong, healthy child who could do all their cleaning. He had heard how the government gave away money to the parents of adopted children. Of course, this was intended for the child's upkeep, but he could steal it for himself and get the child to do all of their housework.

The girl that he chose came from an orphanage in Marseilles. A tall, dark girl called Olive, with strangely coloured eyes that were the exact purple shade of wild lavender.

Coco's father was not disappointed, for the girl proved hard-working. She swept the carpets, mopped the floors and dusted away the cobwebs. She did the washing and the ironing and changed everyone's beds. And in return she was given a bedroom the size of a broom cupboard. In fact, it had once been the broom cupboard until Olive cleared it out. And yet, despite this drudgery, Olive scarcely seemed to notice her chores.

That was partly what Coco found so fascinating about Olive. She had been watching her very carefully ever since the day she arrived. She knew that Olive came from an impoverished background. The orphanage was a poor one and reputed to be quite brutal. There was also the story about the girl's origins: how she had been found abandoned in the port of Marseilles, swaddled in old netting at the bottom of a fishing boat.

Coco had been expecting some kind of guttersnipe, a hardened street child from the slums. Instead she found someone strangely carefree, who seemed not to have any secrets, any hidden fears or desires, except for the fact that she loved to cook.

The first time Olive cooked, Coco's mother was so overcome that she let out a little cry. 'Oh my goodness!' she exclaimed, putting a hand up to her mouth. And then, for the first time in many years, she actually smiled.

After that Olive was asked to cook for them every week, and on these occasions people started dropping by and inviting themselves for supper. They knew that whenever Olive cooked it would be an evening to remember; a time when laughter flowed and friendships were strengthened, and which would leave them feeling things were possible that had not been so before.

As the years passed, stories of this girl and her amazing cookery spread beyond the village to the nearby towns and cities, and even further across France, until eventually they came to the attention of Monsieur Gibier. Monsieur Gibier ran a cookery school in Paris – the most famous cookery school in the world. Monsieur Gibier himself was said to possess the finest taste buds of anyone alive. From a single sip or taste of someone's cooking, he could tell every ingredient, right down to the last pinch of salt.

As soon as he heard tell of this extraordinary girl in the south, Monsieur Gibier paid her a visit. He sampled some of her cooking and what he tasted so astonished him

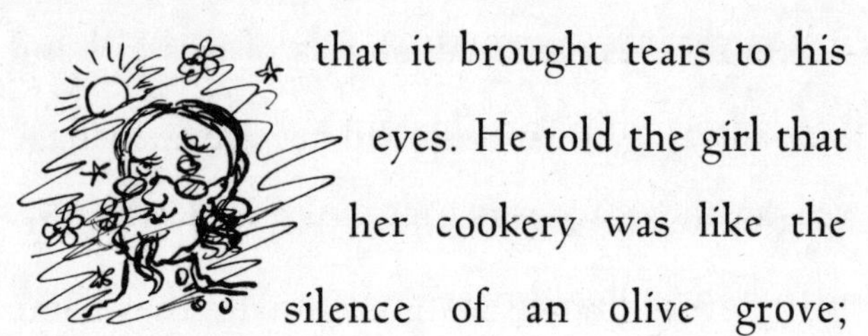

that it brought tears to his eyes. He told the girl that her cookery was like the silence of an olive grove; like a summer breeze through lavender; like a Provençal sunset, when the sky turns crimson above the dusky blue hills. He said that it was the finest cooking he had ever tasted in his life.

At once he offered her a scholarship. She would have full board and lodging and could leave the village for ever, coming to live instead in the city of Paris. And so it was agreed that Olive would travel up there the following term.

The only problem was how to acquire her foster parents' permission. On hearing about the scholarship they instantly refused it. The reason they gave was that they did not believe it to be in Olive's best interests, although the truth was they did not want to lose their miraculous cook. Monsieur Gibier quietly informed them that if they did not let her go, he would report them to the authorities on the charge of adopting a child for slave labour. At once they replied how, on consideration, they thought this would be a wonderful opportunity for Olive and were only too happy to give it their blessing.

To say farewell to everyone in the village, Olive offered to cook one last time. She would prepare an enormous banquet to be laid out in the village square. It would be like a summer fête, with music and dancing going late into the night. Many of the local children volunteered to help set up the banquet, and one of these was Coco.

Coco planned what she would do the moment she heard Olive was leaving. Like her parents, she did not want to see Olive go, although her reasons were quite different.

Partly it was the special envy that comes from feeling left behind. But mostly it was because of a unique quality in Olive that she recognised; a spirit of life which burned brightly at the centre of her being, and which Coco knew she had to extinguish. She was going to make sure that Olive never took up her scholarship.

On the night of the banquet she stole quietly into the kitchen while Olive's back was turned. On the stove a large cauldron of fish stew was bubbling. Olive was busy chopping vegetables. Coco took a jam jar from out of her pocket and unscrewed the lid. Inside were a hundred specimens of a certain locally grown toadstool. It was called the 'Witch's Cap' and was so called on account of its pointed black head, which resembled the traditional hat of a witch. The toadstool's effects were similar to those of severe food poisoning and were invariably deadly; for it was Coco's plan to murder the entire village and make it look as if Olive were responsible. Quite what would happen to Olive, Coco was not sure, though she was in no doubt that Olive would lose her scholarship. She would also never be allowed to cook professionally again.

Coco had always been obsessed with the Witch's Cap toadstool. She did not know why but it often featured in her dreams, especially her nightmares. She could not remember when she had first heard about it but, in fact, it was many years ago, during that time when she was locked in the cellar.

That night she had lain on the cellar floor, huddled into a little ball. She had tried not to make a sound, since in the dark any sound is terrifying, even when it is your own. She had her eyes tight shut, trying desperately to fall asleep, when she suddenly heard a noise. It was the sound of a match flaring, and in the darkness she saw a flame.

The silhouetted form of a woman stood behind it. The woman was about the same size and shape as her mother and so at first Coco's heart leapt, thinking she was about to be released. Until the woman brought the light up closer to reveal it was not her mother, but the most hideous face she had ever seen. The wispy yellow flame lit it dimly from below, making the vision seem all the more macabre. The skin was deathly pale but smothered in rouge, and the mouth was painted in brightly coloured lipstick. It looked like the face of a long-dead corpse that had been covered in thick make-up. She wore no pointed hat, nor was she carrying a broomstick, and yet Coco had no doubt that she was looking at a witch.

'Coco?' said the witch softly. 'Coco?' Her voice was dry and faintly rasping.

Coco felt a hand touch her hair and let out a scream.

'Shh, don't be afraid,' said the witch gently. 'I'm your friend, and I'm here to help you. I'm going to tell you a secret.'

The witch began speaking to her in a soft, hypnotic tone. She told her about the local woods and how there was a certain toadstool growing there that Coco had to find. One day, she said, this toadstool would change her life for ever.

If the witch said anything else, then Coco did not remember it, for soon afterwards she awoke to find her mother standing in the doorway at the top of the cellar stairs.

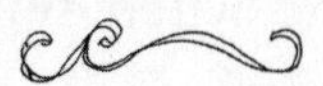

Whether or not the witch was real, Coco never found out. She tried her best not to think about it and later blotted out all memory of that time in the cellar. But she did not forget about the toadstool, and the night before the banquet, it came to her in a dream.

She woke in the dead of night, got out of bed and crept softly downstairs. She took a torch, an old jam jar and a pair of heavy-duty gloves. She packed these into her bag and then set off down the hillside into the woodland below.

Coco foraged there for several hours, until the first light of dawn. She was on the brink of giving up when at last she found them: a whole rash of Witch's Caps growing in the shade of an old elm tree. They were tiny, the size of an acorn, with pointed black heads. She picked over a hundred, just to make sure, and collected them inside the jam jar. This would then be emptied into the fish stew once Olive's back was turned.

On the day of the banquet, all seemed to go according to Coco's plan, until the moment came to empty the jar. For no sooner had she done this than Olive turned round.

'Mmm,' said Coco, inhaling deeply. Hurriedly, she stirred the little toadstools into the stew. 'How delicious! What a treat everyone's in for!'

Olive stared at her in silence. From the look in her eyes, Coco feared that she had been caught red-handed.

'You shouldn't stir it,' said Olive eventually.

'The flavours need to steep.'

'Oh, silly me!' Coco laughed shrilly to cover her relief. 'I'm so sorry, I was only trying to help.' She paused a moment, then added impulsively, 'You know, I've always thought of us as sisters.'

There was a silence.

'Thank you, Coco,' said Olive quietly. 'So have I.'

'And I think you're such an amazing person. You're going to be so famous one day!'

Olive frowned slightly. 'Do you think so?' she said.

'Of course! In the village at least – no one's ever going to forget you after tonight!'

When the fish stew was finally ready, Olive

ladled it into bowls and Coco and the other children took them out to the hungry villagers. Then, while they ate, Coco went to a quiet corner of the village square, where she waited patiently for the poison to take effect.

It was well into the following day by the time Coco realised her mistake. She had picked the wrong toadstool. The Witch's Cap was identical to another, quite harmless variety of fungus that grew in the same woods. However, by then it was too late, for Olive had already left the village to take up her scholarship in Paris.

Olive studied there until she was seventeen, whereupon she left to go travelling and went on to have many adventures. She worked in some of the best kitchens in the world, in cities as far and wide as New York and Tokyo, Mumbai and Berlin. But it was always Paris that she considered her true home and so it was, many years later, that Olive chose to return there and open up a shop; a little shop on the banks of the river, which she ran together with a cat whose name was Camembert. The shop was called 'Edibles' and Olive, by this time, was known as Madame Pamplemousse.

Chapter Five

Camembert lived with Madame Pamplemousse in an apartment above the shop. They ran 'Edibles' by day and come sundown would often share a bottle of Violet-Petal Wine on their balcony high above the city. At night, Camembert would sometimes sleep in the apartment in an old threadbare armchair, but just as often he would go prowling about the city rooftops.

It had been nearly three weeks since either of them had seen Madeleine. This was not so unusual: there were times when the two of them went travelling, or when Madeleine was on holiday with the Cornichons. But one cold night in January, Camembert met with a cat who told him a certain piece of information.

The cat was a friend of his, a young Blue Burmese who had recently run away from his owner. His owner was a girl called Mirabelle and he had been given to her for Christmas. The Burmese told Camembert how he never much liked the girl, but the food was acceptable, so he had decided to stay. At first Mirabelle treated him perfectly well, he said, until just after Christmas, when her behaviour had changed. Mirabelle began playing nasty tricks on the Burmese, locking him in the cellar and chasing him with a water pistol. On one occasion she had even dropped him into a scalding hot bath.

Over breakfast the next morning, Camembert relayed this story to Madame Pamplemousse.

'It sounds like he did well to get away,' she said, dipping a croissant into her coffee, 'though I have to say, I'm not surprised. Often the nicest-seeming girls can be exceedingly cruel.'

'But there's something else,' said Camembert. 'The Burmese said that one day the girl brought home a box of chocolates. He said they smelt funny, really quite disgusting, but the girl seemed to like them; she kept stuffing them into her mouth. And it was only after eating the chocolates that she turned into a little witch.'

Madame Pamplemousse put down her coffee cup. 'That's interesting,' she said, giving him her full attention.

'I found out where this girl lives and yesterday I followed her.' He paused.

'Go on,' said Madame Pamplemousse.

'She goes to the same school as Madeleine.'

It was soon after this that Madeleine's teacher, Madame Poulet, received a visitor. Two visitors, in fact, for one of them was a woman, dressed in black, and the other was a cat; a thin, white cat with a patch across one eye. The woman sat down opposite Madame Poulet's desk and the cat jumped on to her lap.

As a rule, Madame Poulet did not allow animals into the school. She was about to raise this objection when something in the woman's manner made her falter. Somehow she sensed that this woman could not be told what to do. She was also put off by the woman's eyes, which were the most unusual she had ever seen, being

exactly the same colour as lavender.

'Good morning,' said Madame Pamplemousse. 'I've come to talk to you about Madeleine.'

'Madeleine?' said Madame Poulet. 'Ah yes, of course! A bright girl. Rather quiet, perhaps, but hard-working.' She paused.

Madame Pamplemousse raised an eyebrow. 'But there's a problem?' she asked.

'No, no . . .' said Madame Poulet, obviously meaning the exact opposite.

'Please go on.'

'Well, there have been occasions – rather too frequent in my view – when I've caught Madeleine staring out of the window during lessons.'

'And what's wrong with that?'

'I beg your pardon?'

'Well, perhaps she's only staring out of the window because she's bored or because she's thinking about something more interesting.'

Madame Poulet glared over her spectacles. 'May I ask, Madame, what relation you are to this child?'

'I'm her friend,' said Madame Pamplemousse.

'Her friend? Really?'

This notion did not meet with Madame Poulet's approval. She did not like the idea of a child being friends with a grown woman – it sounded unconventional and smacked of poor discipline.

'Well, Madame,' she said, 'perhaps if Madeleine spent less time daydreaming and more time mucking in with everybody else, then she wouldn't be in the mess she's in now!'

'And what "mess" is that, Madame?'

'Well, first let me be quite clear: there's nothing wrong with child prodigies –'

'Though you, yourself, do not approve of them?'

Madame Poulet flared her nostrils. 'No, Madame, I do not! And I don't know how Madeleine behaves at home but here at school she's quite the little so-and-so! Frankly, I'm surprised she still has any friends, the way she treats them. If they weren't such nice friends, I very much doubt she would. One girl in particular, who's gone out of her way to help her –'

'This girl,' interrupted Madame Pamplemousse. 'Her name wouldn't be Mirabelle, by any chance?'

Madame Poulet looked surprised. 'Why, yes. Do you know her?'

'Only by name.'

Madame Poulet's face brightened at the mention of her favourite pupil. 'Now that's the kind of girl Madeleine should be looking up to,' she said. 'The kind of girl this school can be proud of and whom she's jolly lucky to have as her friend.'

'Just as she's obviously lucky to have so wise and perceptive a teacher,' said Madame Pamplemousse.

For a second, Madame Poulet wondered if the woman was being sarcastic, for there was a slight archness to her tone. But then she decided she was just imagining it and softened at the flattery.

'Why, thank you, Madame,' she said.

There was a sudden, low growl. Madame Poulet looked down in alarm. It had come from the white cat, who until now had not made a sound. Then something happened which Madame Poulet found most unsettling. In response to the growl, the woman laughed as if the cat had just said something funny.

Chapter Six

The names Madame Pamplemousse and Camembert no longer meant anything to Madeleine. She had forgotten that they ever existed, just as she seemed to have forgotten so much lately, ever since the day when she had fainted at school – the same time when she had that peculiar dream.

Certain dreams or nightmares are so powerful that they leave behind an atmosphere; a strong mood that can linger like a bad taste in the mouth. Turning on a bedside light is usually sufficient to dispel it, but for Madeleine it never quite went away. She could still vividly remember that icy bedroom with the sinister babysitter waiting next door.

Soon after the day she fainted, she had been passing a café when she stopped outside the window. Something inside caught her eye: a figure sitting at one of the tables.

She noticed his clothing, which was coloured silver and old-fashioned in style.

Seeming to sense Madeleine watching him, he lowered his newspaper. His face was ghostly white and shaped like a crescent moon, and on seeing Madeleine he smiled.

Madeleine stared in horror, transfixed by this apparition. But then a second later she blinked to find an old lady sitting there instead. She assumed her eyes had been playing tricks with the shadows.

Madeleine had also forgotten quite how she and Madame Bonbon had first met, although Madame Bonbon assured her that it was months ago, soon after Madeleine first moved to Paris. She told Madeleine that she had been the one to discover her great talent, and now she was going to make her a star.

Madame Bonbon had arranged for Madeleine to appear on television, on a live game show called *Cook around the Clock*. The producers were delighted, since they had been trying to get their hands on Madeleine for some time. To publicise the show, they had booked a photo shoot. Madeleine was given a complete makeover. She was dressed in the

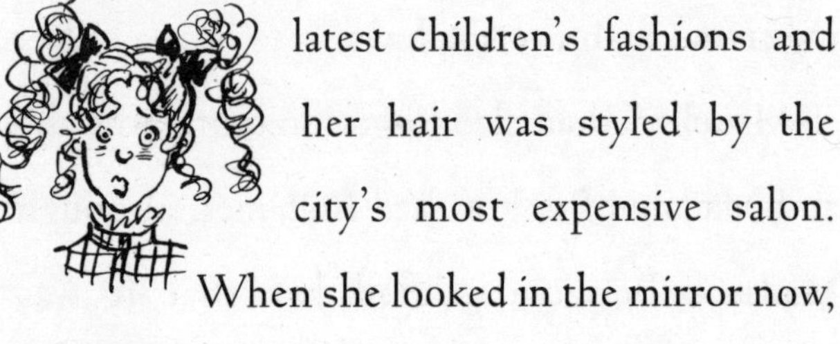

latest children's fashions and her hair was styled by the city's most expensive salon. When she looked in the mirror now, Madeleine hardly recognised her reflection.

In fact, sometimes Madeleine did not even feel like the same person at all. She would stare at herself for ages, trying to remember who that person was, but could find only a strange emptiness; a sense that it was not just her memory that she had lost, but something more vital and irreplaceable. Only Madame Bonbon seemed able to make her feel normal again, by giving Madeleine one of her white chocolate truffles.

'It's because you're changing, Madeleine,' Madame Bonbon reassured her. 'Like a butterfly. You're not that shy little girl who got bullied any more. You're brilliant and beautiful and now everyone will love you.'

Her words certainly seemed to ring true when Madeleine went back to school. From the moment she arrived, Madeleine was treated like a major celebrity. The producers of

Cook around the Clock had invited the whole of Madeleine's year to attend the filming of the show. The headmaster announced this fact proudly to the class and at break-time the canteen was buzzing with excitement. Everyone was coming up to Madeleine, inviting her to sit with them, offering to fetch her lunch, begging to have their picture taken alongside her. People asked if she would sign their workbooks, their lunch boxes, their satchels. There was only one group that hung back conspicuously from the rest.

Mirabelle and her gang were sitting at their usual table. Madeleine stared at them across the room, but not one of them looked up. They were chatting among themselves and appeared quite oblivious to all the commotion around them. To everyone else, Madeleine was the centre of attention,yet they behaved as if she were completely invisible.

'Just ignore them,' said a voice behind her.

Madeleine glanced round to see a boy called Tagine. She knew him slightly, as he was in the same year. Tagine was part of a gang that was quite unusual in the school, since it included girls as well as boys. For this reason Mirabelle called them 'weird', but Madeleine had always liked the look of them. Unfortunately, though, she was too shy ever to go over and say hello.

'They're only pretending to ignore you

because they're jealous. After all, who wouldn't be?' Tagine raised his eyebrows, indicating her new clothes and her hair. His tone was teasing but not unfriendly. 'Still,' he said, 'I'm glad to see you're not hanging around with that bunch any more – I always wondered what you saw in them.' He grinned. 'Good luck with the contest!'

Cook around the Clock was filmed live before a studio audience. The audience consisted mostly of children from Madeleine's school, although the Cornichons had also been invited. Monsieur Cornichon was in a foul temper. He had never liked the idea of

Madeleine taking part in the show and had only agreed to it because his wife insisted. At least, she had said, it meant that Madeleine was cooking again. For the past month now Madeleine seemed to have lost all interest in cookery, staying in bed at weekends and never coming down to the kitchen. When they nervously asked her how things were at school, she replied that they couldn't be better.

'But surely you must be proud of her?' said Madame Cornichon.

'Of course I am!' her husband grumbled.

'Then what's wrong?'

'I don't know. Just a bad feeling.'

'But at least she's smiling again. And she looks so pretty with her new clothes and hair!'

'That's exactly what I'm worried about.'

'What do you mean?'

He shrugged. 'Something's different. She's not the same.'

His wife looked at him wistfully. 'She's growing up,' she said. 'I know it seems sudden, but it had to happen one day.'

'Don't be ridiculous! I mean, she's not herself. Look, don't take this the wrong way, but Madeleine and I used to work together –'

'What's that supposed to mean?' she snapped.

'Nothing, but when you work with someone in the same kitchen –'

'Are you suggesting you know her better than I do?'

'Of course not!' he protested.

But at that point someone told them to be quiet as the show was about to begin.

Cook around the Clock's bouncy theme tune began playing. An usher guided Madeleine out on to the stage. The lights were dazzling. She could barely see the audience but heard their applause as a massive roar.

The presenter introduced the rules of the contest. Either side of the stage there were two kitchens, one painted orange and the other blue. Each kitchen had been stocked with a set of mystery ingredients. Using these ingredients, the two contestants had just thirty minutes in which to prepare a finished recipe. The winner would then be judged by a panel of celebrity guests. The presenter went on to introduce the first contestant and as he spoke her name, Madeleine looked up in shock.

It was Madame Bonbon's idea. She had persuaded the producers that this was the best way to show off Madeleine's unique abilities: to pit her against a child her own age, just an ordinary girl with no special talent, but one brave enough to compete against the young 'gastronomic star'. The girl she had suggested was Mirabelle.

The sight of Mirabelle so disarmed Madeleine that, for a moment, she quite forgot where she was. When the presenter introduced her, she did not understand what he was saying. All that she could hear was the raucous shrieking from Mirabelle's friends; a sound that took her right back to the canteen at school.

Her disorientation continued when the studio clock started ticking and it was several minutes before Madeleine realised that the competition had begun. She now had less than half an hour in which to prepare her finished recipe.

Madeleine stared nervously at the ingredients laid out before her. There were onions, shallots, garlic, celery, potatoes, lemons, ginger, spinach, tomatoes, butter, cream, goat's cheese, Gruyère cheese, puff pastry, lentils, pasta, vinegar, green olives, anchovies, vegetable stock, white wine, spices, fresh tarragon and a large fillet of raw salmon.

Earlier, in her dressing room, Madeleine had received a present. It was a box of truffles from Madame Bonbon, with a note wishing her good luck. Madeleine had eaten one immediately and so had felt blissfully confident as she walked out on to the stage. But now, faced with these ingredients, all that confidence fell away. The effects of the truffle had worn off, leaving her in a state of horrific anxiety; for that was when Madeleine realised that she had forgotten how to cook.

However, it was not just that she had forgotten how to cook a particular recipe. In the past, this happened all the time, but that had never seemed to matter. In trying to recall a recipe she would often come up with something better. Recipes had a way of linking together, mysteriously, like a network of hidden pathways. Her deep feeling for such pathways formed the basis of her technique. But now all that was missing, as if she had lost her intuition, as though her very talent had somehow been removed.

Just then she heard a burst of laughter. The audience were all watching Mirabelle, who was doing something to amuse them. She was cooking at top speed, slamming pans on the stove, chopping all sorts of ingredients and dropping them into a pot. She did this quite randomly and without any show of skill, but

Cook Around
the

that was obviously the point. She was making a mockery of the whole competition. The audience were loving it. In that uncanny way of hers, Mirabelle seemed to have got them all on her side. Madeleine knew she would soon have them laughing at her. She would show the world what a sad misfit Madeleine really was: a child prodigy without any talent.

Madeleine turned away from the cameras and reached into her pocket. She grabbed a fistful of truffles and stuffed them into her mouth. And then, to the surprise of the audience and everyone watching at home, Madeleine collapsed, fainting, with a crash.

Chapter Seven

For a long time it seemed to Madeleine that she was floating through darkness. She had been half sleeping, drifting in and out of consciousness, but as she awoke fully the darkness became suffocating. She tried to move her arms and legs but discovered that they were bound. Her whole body seemed to be shrouded in some kind of covering. The claustrophobia was unbearable and she would have begun struggling had she not heard a sound.

It came distantly, as if from another room; the echoing click of heels on a hard tiled floor. They were stepping quickly and, as she lay there listening, they came closer, until it seemed they were only a few metres away. Abruptly the footfalls stopped. The next thing Madeleine knew, the covers were being ripped from her face.

The Moon Man loomed over her, grinning his cruel smile. Up close she could see

how shiny and greasy his face was with its coating of white make-up. His eyes were dark and fathomless, like pools of black treacle.

Suddenly he reached down to grip Madeleine tightly about the waist. He lifted her over his shoulder and strode out through the door. He carried her into the adjoining room, the great hall that she had spied before. It had a high, vaulted ceiling and tall windows looking out on to a starry night sky. At the far end a fire was burning in the hearth and a woman stood beside it. She turned round as they approached, motioning for the Moon Man to put Madeleine down. It was Madame Bonbon.

'Hello, Madeleine,' she said. 'I hope your journey here wasn't too tiring?'

With her back to the fire, her face was cast mostly in silhouette; only her eyes could be seen gleaming through the shadows.

'Where am I?' asked Madeleine.

'In my true home. Somewhere I found when I was only a child, not much older than you are now.'

As she was speaking she moved closer, to run her fingers through Madeleine's hair.

'There is a kind of mould,' she said, 'which grows only on the walls of caves and damp places underground. Witches call it Silver Moonshine and from ancient times they have used it as a means of travel here – to the spirit world.' She paused to smile. 'I put it in my chocolates.'

Madeleine shut her eyes tightly, shaking her head. 'This isn't real,' she said out loud. 'It's only a dream!'

'No, Madeleine, it's no dream. You are somewhere quite real. And a part of you has always been here, ever since you first tasted my chocolates. That day I found you in the cathedral, do you remember?'

With these words it was as though she drew aside a curtain, as if Madeleine's mind were a darkened room and she was letting in the sunlight. It was with horror that Madeleine now recalled every detail she had forgotten. She remembered where she had been going that day: she was on her way to see Madame Pamplemousse. Until now, all memory of her had been erased from Madeleine's mind.

But in the act of remembering there came a sudden flash of intuition. From the beginning, none of it had been coincidence. That meeting in the cathedral had been planned. Madame Bonbon had followed her there, just as she had known the reason why Madeleine was crying.

'It was you!' Madeleine cried. 'You were using her – you made Mirabelle bully me!'

Madame Bonbon nodded approvingly.

'That's very clever of you, Madeleine. And girls like Mirabelle can be easily led. You were much more difficult. But it was your great weakness, don't you see? Your desire to be ordinary, just like everybody else. And now that's exactly what you are.'

'What do you mean?'

Madame Bonbon tipped her head to one side. 'But can't you tell? Surely you felt it on television?'

'No!' Madeleine whispered.

Madame Bonbon nodded slowly. 'That's right, Madeleine. I took away your talent.'

'But you can't!' Madeleine cried. 'No one can do that! It's not possible!'

'Oh, but there's a great deal which is

possible, thanks to the power granted me by the spirits of this realm.'

She nodded respectfully to the Moon Man, who responded with an enigmatic smile.

'But, you see, I had to do it, because you have something I need. A certain piece of information. Just a tiny thing really, but in return for it, I promise to give you back everything I stole.' She paused a moment, then added quietly, 'I want to know how she travels through time.'

There was a long silence.

'I d-don't know what you're talking about,' Madeleine stammered.

'Don't lie to me,' Madame Bonbon said coolly, with a distinct note of warning. 'You know exactly what I'm talking about. I'm going to ask you a second time. Where does Madame Pamplemousse keep the time machine, and how does it work?'

Madeleine gave no answer, though inwardly she despaired. She understood then just how badly she had been used. But it was all her own fault, her own weakness that had led her into this trap. It was no surprise Madeleine should lose her talent, since she did not deserve it. Nor did she deserve the faith that the Underground had placed in her. But that was also the reason why Madeleine would never betray their secret, because that faith was now the only hope she had left.

'I don't know what you're talking about,'

she said again, but this time with defiance.

Madame Bonbon's face showed no emotion, her eyes shining darkly in the firelight. There was a brief pause before she nodded to the Moon Man, who picked Madeleine up and hurled her straight through the window.

Chapter Eight

Madeleine crashed through the glass, shattering it into a million tiny fragments. For a split second she hung suspended in empty space, the glass shards about her glimmering like the stars above her head.

Madeleine had been thrown from the high window of a castle. The castle was tall, shining white and made entirely out of marble. Far below, the castle was surrounded by a moat of dark water and it was towards this moat that Madeleine began falling.

She shot down like a dead weight, hitting the surface with a giant splash. Then she carried on dropping downwards, going deep into the murky blue. She drifted down slowly until she reached the moat's bed. It was covered with smooth sand, like the bottom of a fish tank. Sitting there, on a lone rock, was a woman. Or at least, the top part of her was a woman; the lower half was that of a fish. She had long, seaweed-green hair that drifted lazily about her head. The Mermaid was combing it with a fish-bone, but at the sight of Madeleine she stopped. The Mermaid smiled. She had a thin, delicately boned face, with transparently pale skin. Her eyes were slit-pupilled and oily like a reptile's. They also looked somewhat frenzied and it occurred to Madeleine that she was not really smiling but baring her teeth, which were tiny and razor sharp like the teeth of a piranha.

In a single motion the Mermaid sprang up and uncoiled her tail. She hovered before Madeleine with her tail gently rippling, then it began beating faster as she propelled herself through the water.

With all her strength Madeleine kicked up from the moat's bed. She pummelled the water furiously in a frantic doggy-paddle. She managed to climb but with awful slowness, while the Mermaid's sleek form swam ever closer towards her. She would have gained on her completely had it not been for a long root that Madeleine saw growing out of the bank. It dipped down into the water and Madeleine grabbed hold of it, using it to haul herself up on to the ground.

Just as she did so, the Mermaid's head burst out of the water. She opened her mouth to shriek; a sound so shrill and piercing that it might have shattered glass. Madeleine picked herself up and began running.

She ran to the nearby forest that surrounded the castle. A dense mist hung over the trees and she could hardly see her way, just the dark silhouettes of the tree trunks immediately in front of her. The trunks were long and spindly and grew sinuously about each other like the bodies of snakes. At times it looked as if they were moving, although this could have been just an illusion created by the drifting trails of mist. Madeleine also thought she could hear whispering. It was only faint but it was all around her and seemed to be coming from the trees. However, when she stopped to listen, the whispering would stop as well.

Just then she heard another sound and Madeleine froze still. It was the sound of footsteps coming through the forest. Madeleine dived down out of sight.

Ahead of her there was a clearing, a wide circle in the trees, and moving across it she could see two figures: a woman and a cat. The woman wore black and the cat was wearing an eyepatch.

'Madame!' whispered Madeleine.

Neither of them seemed to hear her.

'Madame!' She tried again. '*Madame!*' she hissed louder. '*It's me, Madeleine!*'

They stopped dead in their tracks. The woman looked about quizzically, squinting through the mist. Madeleine stepped out from her hiding place.

'Madeleine!' cried Madame Pamplemousse.

She opened her arms wide and Madeleine ran towards them.

'Oh, Madame!' Madeleine gasped. 'I'm so glad to see you!'

Madame Pamplemousse hugged her tight. Camembert joined in with the embrace, nuzzling his head against Madeleine's leg while purring affectionately.

'I'm sorry,' said Madeleine. 'It's all my fault! I've put us all in terrible danger!'

'Hush now,' said Madame Pamplemousse soothingly. 'There's no need to panic.'

Madeleine glanced up. 'Then there's a way out of here? We can escape?'

Madame Pamplemousse nodded. 'But it's not going to be easy. I'm afraid there is only one way out of here, Madeleine.'

'How?'

'We have to give Madame Bonbon what she wants.'

Seeing the shocked expression on Madeleine's face, Madame Pamplemousse laughed.

'Of course, I don't mean we're really going to tell her! I mean we're going to trick her. Listen . . .' She lowered her voice, speaking softly in Madeleine's ear. 'Madame Bonbon is very clever and so the lie we're going to tell her has to be a good one. It has to be very close to the truth, do you understand?'

Madeleine nodded.

'So now I want you to tell me the truth.

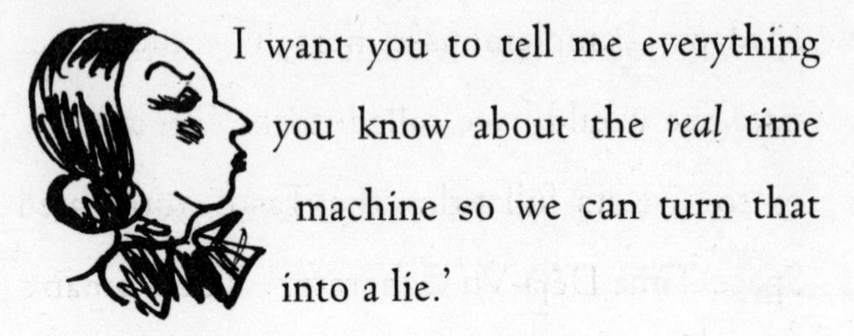

I want you to tell me everything you know about the *real* time machine so we can turn that into a lie.'

Madeleine frowned slightly. 'But why are you asking me?'

'Because it has to be in your own words, silly! I told you, it's got to sound like the truth!'

There was a pause.

'Come on, Madeleine,' she said briskly. 'Quick as you can!'

But still Madeleine did not reply.

It was her use of the word 'machine' that had confirmed Madeleine's suspicions. She had referred to the 'time machine', a term

Madame Pamplemousse herself would never use. She would have called it 'the Generator', or to give its full title, 'the Taste-Automated Space-Time Déjà-Vu Generator'. The woman's questioning was suspicious, but it was actually Camembert who had first raised her alarm – or the creature who looked like Camembert. It was the way he had greeted her so affectionately, nuzzling her and purring. In many cats this might have been perfectly normal behaviour, but in Camembert it was completely out of character.

Madeleine tried to look as if she were recalling a memory. 'All I remember is what you told me the first time we went travelling –'

'Yes?'

'When we were in ancient Rome, you said the machine was essentially classical in design . . .' She trailed off.

'Yes?' said the woman. 'Go on, Madeleine.'

'We never went to Rome,' said Madeleine coldly.

The woman stared back at her with a face equally cold. Her eyes, Madeleine now saw, were not those of Madame Pamplemousse at all. They were beady and lifeless, like the glass eyes of a doll.

'I've heard it said that imitation is the greatest form of flattery,' came a voice through the mist, 'but don't you think this is taking it a little too far?'

The woman turned sharply towards the direction of the voice. And there, coming through the trees on the fringes of the clearing, were the real Madame Pamplemousse and Camembert.

A second later and the two doppelgängers vanished out of sight. Camembert's impersonator became the Moon Man while Madame Pamplemousse's image morphed back into that of Madame Bonbon.

Madame Pamplemousse stopped in the centre of the clearing and for a long moment she and Madame Bonbon appraised each other in silence.

'Hello, Coco,' said Madame Pamplemousse eventually.

'Hello, Olive,' Madame Bonbon replied, giving an odd, girlish smile. 'I must say, I'm impressed. I would have thought myself quite unrecognisable after all these years.'

'But in other ways you haven't changed,' said Madame Pamplemousse, 'and there are ways of seeing that have nothing to do with the eyes.'

Madame Bonbon laughed. 'Well, you haven't changed at all. Is the elixir of youth, by any chance, one of your delicacies?'

Madame Pamplemousse shook her head. 'I'm sorry, Coco,' she said.

'Sorry for what?'

'For the way you truly look, and the reason why you must hide yourself behind this illusion.'

On hearing this, Madame Bonbon's expression briefly registered some emotion. It was only for an instant: a look of anger, or perhaps sadness, playing briefly across her face.

'I don't want your pity, Olive,' she said huskily. 'And I'm not ashamed of the way I look.'

Once again her appearance changed. Madame Bonbon's image vanished and in its place stood the most hideous apparition. Her body had contracted, shrinking from its ample form to become thin and emaciated. Her face, meanwhile, now resembled that of a mummified head. The skin was sickly pale and stretched across the bones, with hollow cheeks and a mouth set into a perpetual grimace. Her eyes, however, had not changed, and stared darkly from out of their sockets.

Madeleine recoiled from the sight in horror. But she did not move far, for the Moon Man stood behind her and gripped her tightly about the neck. She cried out.

'Don't worry, Madeleine,' Madame Pamplemousse called across to her. 'You're going to be all right, I promise. And by the way, hello.' She sent her a special smile. 'It's very good to see you, even if it has to be in this backwater.'

'Backwater!' cried Madame Bonbon. 'Do you realise where you are?'

'Unfortunately, yes,' replied Madame Pamplemousse. 'On one of the lower levels of the spirit realm. I've been to worse, though judging by what it's done to you, there must be a lot of evil here.'

'You're envious!' cried Madame Bonbon, gazing at her in wonder. 'I never would have believed it: that you would envy *me* for turning out to be the more powerful witch!'

'Witch!' Madame Pamplemousse practically spat out the word. 'I'm sorry to disenchant you, Coco. I am a *cook* and, if you must, an artist, but I would never describe myself as a witch.'

Madame Bonbon smiled slyly. 'But I know what it really is, Olive. Your greatest creation:

The Most Incredible Edible Ever Tasted. I know its true name – who apart from another witch could ever tell you that?'

Camembert growled, as if raising an objection.

'And what do you call this,' she hissed, jabbing a finger in his direction, 'if not your witch's familiar?'

'I call him by his name,' said Madame Pamplemousse, 'which is Camembert. And though he certainly is a close friend, I would hardly call him my "familiar".'

'Don't patronise me!' Madame Bonbon screamed.

Her voice reverberated around the clearing, seemingly echoed by the trees, for just then they began to whisper. From the darkness of the forest came the soft hissing of voices. It wasn't possible to hear what they were saying, since all that could be heard was the suggestion of words. Their tone, however, was clear: the sound of mounting fury that grew steadily louder. It rose to become deafening, a fierce chattering all around, until Madame Bonbon raised her hand, when abruptly it ceased.

'Now then, Olive,' she said brightly. 'Earlier you remarked how you had travelled to worse reaches of the spirit realm.' She smiled. 'I doubt that, as you will soon discover to your cost. Or, alternatively, I will give you a chance to spare yourself and your friends by answering a simple question.'

Madame Bonbon paused.

'I want to know how you travel through time.'

She locked eyes with Madame Pamplemousse then – a look of pure challenge. Madame Pamplemousse held her gaze but made no reply.

Madeleine knew that it was hopeless. Madame Pamplemousse would never tell her, for there was no limit to the harm Madame Bonbon might do with such a secret. And even if she did tell her, they had no guarantee that Madame Bonbon would actually release them. Either way they would be imprisoned here for ever.

But then she heard a voice; a gruff, guttural-sounding voice that seemed both strange and familiar. Though she had heard it many times before, until now Madeleine had never understood what it was saying.

'You will find what you're looking for in a café in Montmartre,' said Camembert. 'Its name is the Café of Lost Time.'

Everyone stared at him in astonishment. Madame Pamplemousse looked horrified.

'No, Camembert!' she whispered. 'You mustn't tell her! Be quiet!'

Camembert looked up and shrugged. 'We have no choice,' he said. 'The owner of the café is called Monsieur Moutarde,' he carried on to Madame Bonbon. 'Tell him that I sent you. And there are certain ingredients that you will need to bring with you.'

Camembert explained how the Generator worked, converting specific flavours into locations in time and space.

'And one more thing.' He paused.

'Yes?' she said impatiently.

'Our special code,' he replied. 'The word "mirror".'

There was a long silence.

'Well,' said Madame Bonbon. 'Thank you, Camembert. I'm glad to find you more amenable than your mistress.'

'She's not my mistress,' he growled.

'If you insist. However, I'm sorry to inform you that I will not be releasing you after all. At least not yet, until I have confirmed that what you're telling me is the truth. So, if you excuse me, now I'll be leaving you in the company of my associate here.'

She bowed towards the Moon Man, who responded with an elaborate flourish.

'Until we meet again,' said Madame Bonbon, vanishing into the mist.

Chapter Nine

Later that day, in Montmartre, at the Café of Lost Time, Monsieur Moutarde received a customer. She was a small, skele-tally thin woman who wore a great quantity of make-up. However, rather than disguise her ugliness, this only made it appear all the more grotesque. At first sight, Monsieur Moutarde was quite taken aback, although being a perfect gentleman he pretended not to notice.

'What can I get you, Madame?' he asked.

Madame Bonbon stared at him in silence, her eyes darkly piercing. Monsieur Moutarde smiled, gesturing to the café bar.

'A coffee, perhaps? Or something stronger?'

'Your friends are in danger,' she said suddenly. She spoke quietly, in a dry, rasping voice. 'If you ever wish to see them again then you must do exactly as I say. You have a device here called the Generator, and I wish to use it.'

Monsieur Moutarde looked confused. 'Generator?' he said, frowning. 'That's not a drink I'm familiar with. May I suggest a glass of cognac instead?'

'Don't play with me!' she snarled. 'I mean what I say. I have your friends held captive. They are counting on you to save them. That is why they told me where to find you and why they gave me your special code –'

'I'm sorry, Madame, but I really have no idea –'

'The code "mirror",' she interrupted.

On hearing this word, Monsieur Moutarde's expression froze. He remained silent for some time and when he finally spoke again, it was in a quite different tone.

'To what precise time do you wish to travel, Madame?' he asked softly.

Madame Bonbon told him what he asked and then removed a hand from her pocket. In her palm was a single lemon bonbon. Moutarde took this with a short nod and then went over behind the bar to what looked like a large, silver espresso coffee machine – for this was, in fact, the Generator.

The Taste-Automated Space-Time Déjà-Vu Generator was a complex device but its main principle was quite simple. It produced a liquid whose flavour gave you a strong feeling of déjà vu; the sense you were reliving an especially vivid memory or dream. The Generator then tricked the universe so that this feeling became reality. The liquid would actually transport you through time and space.

On top of the Generator there was a large silver funnel, into which Monsieur Moutarde dropped the lemon bonbon. He then adjusted several dials and turned on a switch. There was a loud hissing and a cloud of steam issued from out of the machine. At the same time a thin dribble of hot liquid was dispensed into a cup. He gave this to Madame Bonbon together with a small Thermos flask.

'The flask contains coffee,' he told her. 'It will bring you back to the present time when you wish to return. And this,' he said, handing her the cup. 'This will take you to your chosen destination.'

She stared at it in silence.

'Hurry, Madame!' he whispered. 'You don't want to let it cool.'

Madame Bonbon tipped her head back and drank the liquid down. Almost at once it took effect. At first everything in the room became still, as if it had been captured in a snapshot. But this image began revolving, turning faster and faster like a merry-go-round. The room became a whizzing blur, then just a wheel of spinning colour. As it spun faster, so the colours grew darker, until eventually they turned to black.

Suddenly, Madame Bonbon realised that the spinning had stopped. The café had disappeared and she was standing in darkness.

After a time, she reached into her pocket for a match. She struck it and the match flared. Gradually she became aware that she was somewhere underground, in a cavernous, dank space. The air was cold and damp and smelled strongly of mildew. Madame Bonbon struck another match and that was when she saw the child.

She was lying on the floor, her body curled up tight into a little ball. Madame Bonbon was so shocked by the sight of her, at how vulnerable she seemed, that tears began pricking at her eyes. For the figure that she saw lying there was herself as a seven-year-old child.

'Mama?' said the girl, sleepily raising her head. She was wet through, with filthy clothing and her cheeks black with soot. Slowly the girl's eyes grew accustomed to the light and then they became wide with fear.

'Coco?' whispered Madame Bonbon. 'Coco?' She reached out her hand.

The girl backed away but Madame Bonbon came closer, making her scream.

'Shh, don't be afraid,' said Madame Bonbon softly. 'I'm your friend, and I'm here to help you. I'm going to tell you a secret.'

Then she whispered to the child, who was trembling with fright. She told her all about a certain fungus, called the Witch's Cap

toadstool, that grew in the nearby woods. One day, she said, this toadstool would change her life for ever.

'But listen to me, Coco,' she said. 'You must be very careful to make sure you pick the right one, for there is another kind, very similar, that is not poisonous at all –'

She broke off in mid sentence. For Madame Bonbon had just experienced the most extraordinary déjà vu.

She remembered then, with sharp clarity, how she had first heard about the Witch's Cap. It was now – this very moment – when she was seven years old. She remembered being locked in the cellar and how frightened she had been. And she remembered meeting the witch. It was a memory so terrible that she had since blocked it from her mind. But now she was reliving it, at the very same moment as it first happened in time.

Soon after inventing the Generator, Monsieur Moutarde discovered that it held a potential danger. He realised this quite by chance shortly before travelling back to his childhood. Travelling to your own past, he reasoned, was actually highly dangerous, since it could give rise to what he called a 'Mirror Déjà Vu'. And it was just such a Mirror Déjà Vu that Madame Bonbon was now experiencing, because the universe was confused. It could not decide which was real: the woman experiencing the memory from when she was a child, or that same child experiencing what would later become the memory. However, as the universe generally tends to err on the side of life, it chose the child, and the woman vanished away altogether.

Chapter Ten

No sooner had Madame Bonbon disappeared from Paris than Madeleine found herself waking up there. She was in a television studio, surrounded by anxious-looking producers.

'She's awake!' one of them cried, and a loud cheer went around.

A taxi was arranged to take Madeleine back home, but on his way the driver was instructed to make a small detour via the Café of Lost Time. Madame Pamplemousse met them outside the door. She asked the driver to leave the meter running, as she had something to give Madeleine and they would only be gone a moment.

One of the great advantages of time travel is the ability to go on long holidays and return only seconds later. Madame Pamplemousse thought Madeleine would be in need of relaxation, so she took her to an era in Earth's history known as the Late Devonian Period,

350 million years ago. It was a time of great tranquillity and mild, tropical climates, long before the dinosaurs had evolved.

During the timeless days, Madeleine swam in the ocean or lazed in the sun. Or sometimes she would go off exploring across the plains with Camembert. In the evenings, however, the three of them would always meet to dine out under the stars.

It was over dinner that Madame Pamplemousse told Madeleine how they had found her. Camembert's friend, the Blue Burmese, had led Camembert to the sweet shop, where he had stolen a box of the white chocolate truffles. Madame Pamplemousse had then extracted the special ingredient: the silvery-white mould known as Silver Moonshine. That was when she guessed Madame Bonbon's true identity, for she remembered this mould from her childhood in Provence. It grew down in the cellar, in a house she and Coco had once shared.

'Long ago,' said Madame Pamplemousse, 'when I last saw Coco, she attempted to commit an act of great evil. If she had succeeded, it would have cost many people their lives.'

'What did she do?' asked Madeleine.

'She tried to poison my cooking. But fortunately, her plan failed, for the toadstools she used were not poisonous at all. The only damage she did was to give my stew an unwarranted flavour of mushrooms. But I knew that was why she wanted the Generator: to undo her mistake.'

'But weren't you afraid she might succeed?'

Madame Pamplemousse shook her head. 'Whatever happened back then merely happened over again. Or rather, it only happened once but Coco was forever doomed to repeat it.'

But even with her gone, Madeleine secretly feared that Madame Bonbon's spell was not broken. She never mentioned these concerns, although one evening Madame Pamplemousse broached the subject of her returning to school.

'I understand you may not wish to discuss this, Madeleine,' she said, 'but there's something you ought to know.'

Camembert miaowed. Since leaving the spirit world, Madeleine had not been able to understand him but Madame Pamplemousse translated. She explained about Mirabelle's cruelty to the Blue Burmese.

'But he says the Burmese always knew she was a bad business. He never liked her that much to begin with.'

Camembert miaowed some more.

'He says he plans to get his revenge. Being dropped in hot baths will be the least of her problems.' Madame Pamplemousse broke off.

'That won't be necessary!' she told him

firmly. 'Although he may be right,' she said to Madeleine. 'Mirabelle may have been under Coco's spell, and will have no memory of what happened, but I'm afraid you won't find her significantly changed.'

Madeleine closed her eyes, burying her face in her hands.

'I'm sorry,' said Madame Pamplemousse gently. 'But I do promise you: the bullying will stop.'

'No, it won't,' said Madeleine. 'How could it? I'm too much of a coward.'

'On the contrary, I have always thought you remarkably brave. But the truth is, Mirabelle and Coco are two of a kind. In both cases their power lies in turning people against themselves.

Mirabelle made you feel bad for being special, by making you feel different. Well, Madeleine, I have to say, you *are* different, but that's nothing to be ashamed of. And as for "fitting in", personally I never have, nor do I intend doing so. But you know,' she paused to smile, 'that has never stopped me having friends.'

When the day finally came for Madeleine to go back to school, it was just as she had been dreading. Coming through the school gates she felt that old twisting in her stomach and the tightness in her chest.

She caught sight of them immediately on the other side of the playground: Mirabelle and her gang. They had seen her too and were already smirking to each other and beginning to sidle over. Madeleine closed her eyes, trying to stop herself from trembling. She tried to recall that brilliant light, the deep quiet and open spaces of the prehistoric Earth. She wished she could escape there now, drink the time-travelling liquid and disappear.

'So?' said a voice curtly. 'What happened to you?'

Madeleine opened her eyes to find Mirabelle with her arms folded, giving her an insolent stare. There was no question after her health, not even a hello. Previously Madeleine would have tried to compensate, fawning all over Mirabelle in an effort to appease her. But this time she just stared back and replied matter-of-factly.

'I fainted,' said Madeleine.

'Well, we could see that!' Mirabelle made a face to approving laughter from the group. 'But we wondered if you faked it, because really you're a liar. Actually you're not such a brilliant cook after all!'

The barb was well chosen and intended to wound. It might easily have done so had Mirabelle said it only minutes earlier. For then it would have been true: since the television show Madeleine had indeed lost all her ability to cook. Until that very moment, when something extraordinary happened: from out of nowhere she suddenly had an idea.

It was an idea for a cookery book. Her first cookery book, whose recipes would all involve the use of fresh herbs. But the recipes' true connection would be subtler, more mysterious, and could only be guessed at through tasting.

Such ideas were rare. They arrived in the mind almost fully formed and yet were themselves the seeds from which other ideas grew. That was when Madeleine knew she had never really lost her talent. It had simply withdrawn out of fear, like a plant in winter, only to come back stronger than before.

She was so delighted to discover this, and so

beguiled by her idea, that for an instant she quite forgot about Mirabelle. She even forgot to be afraid of her and, seeming to sense this, Mirabelle quickly changed tack.

'Anyway, it's cool,' she said, flicking her hair. 'The producers said I'm a natural. They want me to do an advert.'

'What for?' asked Madeleine.

'Chocolate,' she replied.

Madeleine could not help but smile at the irony of this.

'Oh, look, everyone, she's smiling!' said Mirabelle. 'What's so funny, Madeleine? Aren't you going to share the joke?'

Madeleine shook her head.

'Oh dear,' Mirabelle sighed. 'What *are* we

going to do with her?'

She pretended to be disappointed, though Madeleine could tell she was relieved. It must have been a huge threat to her, the prospect of Madeleine becoming a star. Apart from the feelings of envy, it would have severely undermined Mirabelle's authority.

'I'm sorry, Mirabelle,' said Madeleine, 'but I don't have time for this any more.'

'Time?' Mirabelle glared at her. 'Time for what?'

'For playing games.'

'Are we playing?' She looked for confirmation from the other girls. 'Sorry, Madeleine, I don't think so. We're chatting. This is called *having a conversation* – you know, the way normal people do with their friends –'

'But you're not my friends,' said Madeleine quietly.

Mirabelle fell silent. She stared at Madeleine with her eyes boggling and her mouth gaping open. This was the last thing she would ever have expected Madeleine to say and it made any retort impossible. All she could do was disagree and that would look as though she were begging Madeleine to be her friend. So instead Mirabelle just gave a mocking laugh.

But Madeleine found she no longer cared. She turned her back on them all and walked away to a quiet corner of the playground. There she could continue thinking about her cookery book undisturbed.

She did not hear their jeers or any other noises in the playground; for that moment she was perfectly happy just being by herself. But the moment did not last for long, as soon afterwards she was joined by Tagine and his friends.

Epilogue

On the Isle Saint Louis there is no longer a shop called 'Sweet Dreams'. The shop closed after its owner mysteriously disappeared. She left no clue as to her whereabouts and all of the shop's contents vanished at the same time. However, one of the sweets did turn up a short while later.

It was delivered to the office of Madame Poulet at her school. No one knew who sent it, one morning it just arrived on her desk: a rose-coloured chocolate in the shape of a heart, with a message that read simply: *From an admirer.*

The chocolate was filled with a lightly whipped strawberry mousse and another ingredient which was, in fact, a witch's love potion. Its effect was to make you fall in love with whomever you set eyes upon after eating it. In Madame Poulet's case, this was the headmaster.

However, the potion did not act immediately and it was later, during assembly, when it finally took effect. The headmaster was in the middle of a speech when Madame Poulet suddenly clasped her arms about him in a passionate embrace. It was only after hearing the gales of laughter that she remembered where she was.

Camembert later told this story over dinner, for it was he who had delivered the gift. It was a dinner given in Madeleine's honour by Madame Pamplemousse's friends, a secret collective whose members sometimes called themselves the Underground. And suitably enough, the dinner was also held underground, by candlelight, below a café in Montmartre, underneath the streets of the city of Paris.

Have you read Madeleine's other adventures?

Turn the page for an exciting taster of

MADAME PAMPLEMOUSSE
AND HER
Incredible Edibles

Chapter One

In the city of Paris, on the banks of the river, tucked away from the main street down a narrow, winding alley, there is a shop. A small, rather shabby-looking shop with faded paint-work, a dusty awning and dark, smoky windows. The sign above the door reads 'Edibles', as it is a food shop selling all kinds of rare and exotic delicacies. But they are not just rare and they are not just exotic, for this shop belongs to Madame Pamplemousse, and she sells the strangest, the rarest, the most delicious, the most extraordinary, the most incredible-tasting edibles in all the world.

Inside, the shop is cool and musty-smelling, lit only by candlelight. In the flickering shadows, great bunches of sausages and dried herbs, strings of garlic and chilli peppers, and giant salted meats hang from the ceiling. Rows of cheeses are laid out on beds of dark green leaves and all around there are shelves winding up to the ceiling, crammed with bottles and strangely shaped jars.

Underneath the shop, down a winding spiral staircase, at the end of a long, dark corridor, there is a door. A door that is forever kept locked. For it is behind this door that Madame Pamplemousse cooks her rarest delicacy, a delicacy sold in the tiniest little jar with a label upon which nothing is written. The label is blank and the ingredients are a secret, since it is the single most delicious, the most extraordinary, the most incredible-tasting edible of them all.